MICKEY'S MICROPHONE MAGIC

W9-BHX-653

TABLE OF CONTENTS

we make books come alive™

pi **Phoenix International Publications, Inc.**

Chicago • London • New York • Hamburg • Mexico City • Paris • Sydney

Time for adventure! Pack up and sing along!

Press the colored buttons on your microphone in the order you see to hear the toe-tapping tunes!

Pack Up Your Suitcase

Melody: "Pack Up Your Troubles in Your Old Kit Bag"

Pack up your suitcase, leave your cares behind,

And smile, smile, smile!

Who knows what's up ahead for you to find?

Smile through every mile!

What's the use of worrying?

It never was worthwhile.

So pack up your suitcase, leave your cares behind,

And smile, smile, smile!

MINNIE ♥ MOUSE

AIRSPEED
160
140
40
KNOTS
120
60
100 80

MICKEY ♥ MOUSE

CREW

Up in the air or along the boulevard, you can find adventure wherever you go!

Away We'll Fly

Melody: "Come Josephine in My Flying Machine"

Come, Minnie Mouse,

We'll fly over my house,

And it's up we go! Up we go!

Up, up—we always love flying.

Up, up—it's so satisfying.

Just you and me

When we're pilots you see,

Going up, away we'll fly!

Stroll All Around the City

Melody: "Go Round and Round the Village"

Stroll all around the city

And sing this little ditty.

It always sounds so pretty,

From Spain to Singapore!

Travel near, travel far. A song in your heart puts a spring in your step!

London Bridge

London Bridge is standing tall,

Standing tall, standing tall.

London Bridge has seen it all, my fair Minnie!

London Bridge is strong and steady,

Strong and steady, strong and steady,

London Bridge is always ready, my fair Minnie!

Greeting from **London** lots of love Pos...

postcard

wish you were here!

to Mickey

from minnie

♥ love minnie x

to Mickey

from Minnie

The Smile You See

Melody: "The Happy Farmer"

The smile you see—
    It isn't just for me.
I know that I can make it grow just like a tree.
    This smile's for you.
And you can share it, too!
    Just pass it on—
It's never gone. It's always new!

I Feel Shy

Melody: from "The Polovtsian Dances"

I feel shy,
    And I don't know just what to say.
I may whisper softly or
    I may turn my face away.
I need a little time—
    But I know we can find a way.
I will always be your friend.
    I still want to come and play!

Move along as you sing this silly song!

If You're Silly and You Know It

Melody: "If You're Happy and You Know It"

WORRIED · SILLY · GIGGLY · HAPPY · SILLY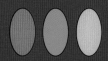

If you're silly and you know it, flap your arms!
If you're silly and you know it, flap your arms!
Stick your tongue out, make a face,
Wiggle all around the place!
If you're silly and you know it, flap your arms!

CRAZY · HAPPY · SLEEPY · SILLY

10

Happy, silly, shy—there are so many ways to feel. That's emotion!

That's EMOTION!

Melody: "Pop Goes the Weasel"

You're up, you're down, you're all around.
Your moods can be in motion!
They stay to play, then slip away—
(POP!) That's emotion!

Come on, gang! We'll hit the trail, then gather round the campfire for these happy camping tunes!

Row, Row, Row Your Boat

Row, row, row your boat
   Gently down the stream.
Merrily, merrily, merrily, merrily,
   Life is but a dream.

Do Your Ears Hang Low?

Do your ears hang low?
    Do they wobble to and fro?
Can you tie them in a knot?
    Can you tie them in a bow?
Can you soar above the nation
    With a feeling of elation?
Do your ears hang low?

The Bear Went Over the Mountain

The bear went over the mountain,

The bear went over the mountain,

The bear went over the mountain

To see what she could see.

We'll Be Comin' Round the Mountain

Melody: "She'll Be Comin' Round the Mountain"

We'll be comin' round the mountain this bright day.

We'll be comin' round to sing and dance and play.

We'll be comin' round the mountain,

We'll be comin' round the mountain,

We'll be comin' to have fun and shout hooray!

By the sea

By the sea, by the sea, by the beautiful sea—
   You and I, you and I, oh how happy we'll be!
I love to be beside your side beside the sea,
   Beside the seaside,
By the beautiful sea!

From up in the mountains to down by the sea, singing along with good friends makes you happy in all kinds of scenery!

I Love the Sea

Melody: "Anchors Aweigh"

I love the oceanside.

I love the sea!

Outdoors on sandy shores,

That's where I want to be!

Waves crashing, splishing, splashing—

Have some fun

Out in the sun with me!

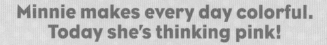

Minnie makes every day colorful.
Today she's thinking pink!

I Dream of Minnie with the Bright Pink Bow

Melody: "I Dream of Jeannie with the Light Brown Hair"

I dream of Minnie with the bright pink bow,

   Wrapped in a rainbow each day from head to toe.

I dream of Minnie with the bright pink bow,

   Dancing with colors from white to indigo.

Roses Are Pink

Melody: "Lavender's Blue"

Roses are pink,
Minnie, Minnie,
Roses are white.
Let's go have fun,
Minnie, Minnie,
All day and night!

You can always count on Minnie for a friendly smile and a happy song. Grab your microphone and sing along!

Two Little Apples

Melody: "Six Little Ducks"

Two little apples on the tree,

One for you and one for me.

In your pack for a snack

Or a treat to go with lunch,

Let's eat together with a crunch, crunch, crunch!

Count with Me

Melody: "Hot Cross Buns"

Count with me!
    One, two, three—
Count just one more,
    One, two, three, four.
Count with me!

Knick Knack

Melody: "This Old Man"

Minnie Mouse, she picked one.

She picked berries just for fun.

With a knick knack paddy whack

Pick a peach or plum:

One, two, three, four, five, six, YUM!

Countdown!

Melody: "When Johnny Comes Marching Home"

Let's all count down from ten to one,

Hurrah, hurrah!

Let's all count down from ten to one,

Hurrah, hurrah!

Let's all count down from ten to one,

And that's the end; our song is done—

And it's 10-9-8-7-6-5-4-3-2-1!

Hot dog! Practice every day,
and you'll get better and
better and better!

I've Been Practicing Piano

Melody: "I've Been Working on the Railroad"

I've been practicing piano.

How I love to play!

I've been practicing piano.

Yes, I do it every day.

Music elevates my spirit—

Playing and singing all day long.

Listen now, oh can you hear it?

It's my favorite song!

My Friend
Mickey's House

Melody: "Old MacDonald"

Up the street is Mickey's house.

Come on pals, let's go!

Let's all visit Mickey Mouse.

Come on pals, let's go!

With a good friend here

And a good friend there,

Here a friend, there a friend,

Everywhere a good friend.

Up the street is Mickey's house.

Come on pals, let's go!

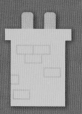

It's time to head home!
Sing along as you go!

Headin' Home

Melody: "Bill Bailey, Won't You Please Come Home"

Let's all go home and play now.

    Let's all go home!

We've been away so long.

    We've traveled far and fast, yes—

Let's slow it down

    And sing this little song!

It's getting late.

    Wow, we're feeling great.

We're ready now to head on home!